Nine Cats: Nine Lives

In The Tall, Narro

Elizabeth S. Deichman

Edited by Veronica Breen Hogle

Aventine Press

Published by Aventine Press
1023 4th Ave #204
San Diego CA, 92101
www.aventinepress.com

ISBN: 1-59330-525-7

Printed in the United States of America

ACKNOWLEDGMENTS

I wish to thank my family and friends for encouraging me to complete this little book about the nine cats and their nine lives while we lived, in our tall, narrow brick house in the City of Buffalo, New York.

I especially want to thank Betty Bates, Joanne Bickel, Barbara Carr, Betty Carr, Jean Millholland, Marjorie Roth and Barbara Smith who carefully read each story and gave me suggestions and moral support. A special thank you to Ann Goldsmith and April Anne Noe who proofread the pages.

I appreciate the skill of Peter F. Sloan, whose pen and ink drawings recapped the essence of each cat's story. I'm grateful to Veronica Breen Hogle for editing the stories and bringing them alive.

Also to Linda Lavid, whose advice and technical assistance brought the project to completion. Their support and enthusiasm made it possible for me to finally write the stories of our nine beloved cats and recap the comfort and joy each one brought into my life.

Elizabeth S. Deichman.

DEDICATION

This book is dedicated in fond memory of my husband:

Henry Andrew Deichman

Who brought the pleasure of cats into my life and their love into our home.

And also in memory of:

Ruth Koch Astmann

Who having declared, "I don't feel comfortable around cats," quickly succumbed to the persuasive charms of Jacob Picasso a cat that refused to believe a person could not love him.

FOREWORD

Cats in our society do not always fare well. The cats in the following stories typify the cats that I see at the shelter on a daily basis. They are like nomads of the desert, wandering through life with their only seeming wish to find a home that will keep and feed them.

So many cats live on this treadmill of life, finding a home, losing a home, finding a new home, and then losing that one too. The cats in these stories, after typical problems cats face in our society, find lifetime homes with a loving couple in a tall, narrow brick house. The love and care they receive is what I wish for every shelter cat, in every shelter, in every town and city in this country.

These fortunate nine cats never needed all their nine lives once they found this wonderful home. My sincere wish is for readers of these stories to commit a small part of their one life to helping the homeless cats in our community. With this help, we will be able to make substantial progress for our friend and companion, the cat.

Barbara S. Carr, Executive Director
Erie County Society for the Prevention of Cruelty to Animals Chair, National Federation of Humane Societies.
March 2008

OUR FAMILY TREE

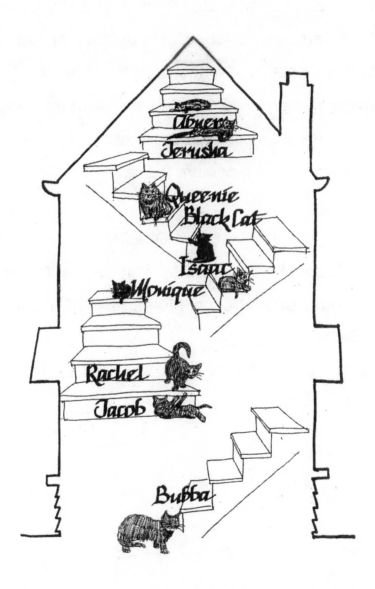

TABLE OF CONTENTS

In The Beginning – Abner O'Grady 1

A Wednesday Night in February – Jerusha Killarney.....11

A Snowy Night – Blackcat..............................23

Aunt Mary's Favorite Dessert – Queenie Cat................31

A Valentine's Day Confession – Queenie Cat...............41

Smoke Got In My Eyes – Queenie Cat.........................47

The Postman Brings A Special Package –
    Queenie Cat...55

My Big Birthday Bash – Abner O'Grady......................63

A Post Script - Queenie Cat 75

From a Home in the Sun to a Home in the Snow –
    Monique...77

My Little World – Isaac Guardian...................................85

County Boy Moves to the City – Jacob Picasso.............95

The Visitor Who Did Not Like Cats – Jacob Picasso...103

A Thank You Letter – Jacob Picasso...........................113

A Wish Comes True – Rachael Louise.......................117

Bubba Comes Back To The Neighborhood – Bubba....129

A Post Script   - Jacob Picasso 139

Did You Know 141

About The Author..............................143

About The Editor...............................145

IN THE BEGINNING

By Abner O'Grady

In Residence: 1967 – 1988

On April 1, 1967, Jerusha Killarney and I were born in Hamburg, a small town south of Buffalo, New York. After we had lived ten weeks with Mama, a man named Henry and his wife Beth came to see us because they heard we were looking for a good home. That very night, they put us into cat carriers. We drove about 30 miles and arrived in the City of Buffalo. The car stopped in front of a tall, narrow brick house with a porch and seven windows in the front.

While they unpacked the car, we waited on the back seat looking out the car window. We could see the house was one of the oldest on the one-way street lined with a variety of tall trees. The brass doorknocker and mailbox gleamed in the light from the streetlamps. Henry carried us up the stairs and placed our carriers on the porch, which was decorated with potted, plump red geraniums and lush green ferns. Crickets were singing and the scent of magnolia perfumed the night air. Henry opened the wide, hand-carved dark door. He picked up my carrier and Beth took the handle of Jerusha's carrier.

We entered the small vestibule leading into a long hallway. Just at that moment, the grandfather clock chimed nine times and made a mellow, soothing sound. I looked up the stairs and noticed the dark wood banister had an ornate swirl at the top. Just as I was wondering what was around the corner of the stairs, Henry and Beth picked up our carriers and brought us into a room with a sofa, armchairs, and a big window with lace curtains. There were also two life-sized giraffes dressed as if they were going to a Fourth of July party.

"Let's get them out of the carriers!" said Beth. Jerusha and I looked at each other. We were nervous in the strange house. Then I took the lead and walked out first, and a few minutes later, Jerusha followed me. The feel of the thick, red carpet with oriental designs felt lovely under our paws. We nudged each other with happiness. I noticed the fireplace right away and envisioned taking long naps in the winter while the snow we had heard about swirled outside.

"Come on, follow me," said Beth in a soothing voice. We walked after her into another room.

"This room is called the library," she said smiling at us. Jerusha went after her and I followed. The shelves were packed all the way up to the ceiling with old books, vases and framed pictures. There was another fireplace.   Big maple leaves tapped gently on the outsides of the twin windows. Framed photos of beautiful felines adorned the walls.

Then we strolled into a third room, which had a handsome glass cabinet full of china, silver and crystal. At the side of the room, I saw narrow steps winding their way to a mysterious place called upstairs.

"This is our dining room," said Henry. He leaned down and scratched our ears.

"Here, come with me!" Beth called to us and we followed her down a step into a fourth room.

"This is the kitchen," she said, filling two china bowls up to the top with chunks of delicious white tuna fish. We sat and ate politely and I noticed a clock in the kitchen chimed every fifteen minutes. I also noticed two more sets of stairs leading up to the mysterious upstairs.

"And that's the cellar down those stairs, where you will find your litter boxes," she added. It was amazing to see so many different staircases in one old house. Later that night, I listened in to the sounds of the house and to Beth and Henry talking.

"I was just thinking of 'Hawaii,' the movie we went to see last night," said Beth to Henry.

"Were you? What were you thinking?"

"The hero and heroine were named Abner and Jerusha." I enjoyed the movie so much, I'd like to call the little female Jerusha."

"Great name," agreed Henry. "How about calling him Abner?" he suggested.

"Oh, how perfect!" said Beth with a huge smile. From that moment on, we were Abner and Jerusha.

In the days that followed, we discovered that the house had nine sets of stairs. There were big rooms and small rooms with soft sofas and beds. A door from the kitchen led out into a courtyard garden kept private by high brick walls. When we became familiar with the house, we often went out into the garden and hid in the ivy watching squirrels, birds, butterflies and bees. We also enjoyed the scent of flowers and the baby catnip plants. We took many naps in the sun and the shade. We listened in as Henry and Beth sat in garden chairs and talked with their friends and visitors.

Life was blissful. Within a year, Jerusha and I had our own three beautiful kittens. We chased them all over the house and up and down the many sets of stairs. When our kittens were older, they went to good homes. Jerusha and I had the house to ourselves again.

Sadly, the Great Cat in the Sky came for my beloved Jerusha when she was only five years old. Still, I lived a long and happy life of over twenty years. I was the first family historian and recording secretary. This office is elected each year and at this writing, Queenie Cat is in line for this position. We hope you will enjoy this collection of simple short stories that tell about the nine cats, each of us longing for a good home. We all found it in the tall, narrow brick house.

When you purchase this little book, you will assist animal shelters to continue to find kind people like Beth and Henry to give good homes to cats. Today, there are many kittens and cats in your local animal shelters. They sit and look out of their cages, hoping the right people will come along. These cats are longing to be taken to a good home, where they will be cared for and loved.

****

A WEDNESDAY NIGHT IN FEBRUARY

By Jerusha Killarney

In Residence: 1967 - 1972

My big love, Abner and I were the first cats to live with Beth and Henry in the tall, narrow brick house on the tree-lined street in the city. Life for us was better than we ever imagined. But for some time, I had been feeling strange and my body had become round and fat. I moved slowly and I was heavy on my feet.

"I think Jerusha's kittens are due any time now," I heard Beth say to Henry one cold winter day.

"Yes," he said. "She's going to have her first litter. Remind me to get a nice box to prepare a bed for her."

"Since it's Ash Wednesday," said Beth, "let's go out to a restaurant for a quick fish dinner with our friends." Before she put on her coat, she put my dear Abner down in the cellar. I was a bit nervous being left alone and I was worried that I saw no bed ready for whatever was going to happen.

"We won't stay too long. We'll bring our friends back for coffee and dessert," Beth told us.

I settled down inside the hall door leading into the vestibule and waited for them to return. But not long after they were gone, I began to feel poorly and had intermittent pains that got harder and harder. I lay on my side and stretched out. Then I felt a huge pressure and I looked down, and there was my brand new tiny kitten. I was licking her when I heard the familiar voices of Beth and Henry plus two other people. I heard the key turning in the lock and the heavy outside door opened. Then Henry pushed the vestibule door inward and hit my back. I let out a sharp meow and he quickly stepped back into the light, and inched the door open.

"Oh, my goodness! She's already had a kitten!" he gasped. Then with great caution, his big feet stepped over me.

"Be careful," he said, as Beth and the two friends followed him. I felt a big pain again, followed by more huge pressure. This time I knew another kitten was on its way.

"Sit down here on the sofa," said Henry to the visitors. "I'm going to get her bed ready." He soon reappeared with a lovely square box, which he padded with soft towels and placed near me in the hallway.

"I'll make the coffee and bring in the dessert," Beth said, heading off towards the kitchen.

Just as the coffee and dessert were served, I felt another huge pressure. The male guest bent his head over to study me.

"This is just marvelous! It's as good as watching Wild Kingdom!" he said.

What could wild kingdom mean I wondered as my insides felt like a balloon? But even with all the pressure, my second kitten was taking a long time to arrive. Beth sat down on the floor and stroked me gently. In a coaxing voice, she talked to me: "Come on, Jerusha, come on, girl! You can do it! I hear you purring and purring."

Her soothing voice gave me confidence. Within a few seconds, in another wave of huge pressure, my second kitten was born. The guests and Henry cheered me on. Then I felt another big pain.

"Oh, I think there is another," said the lady guest. Beth sat at my side, felt my tummy and said,

"I think you're right! Come on Jerusha, you're a great girl. Go for three!" In what seemed like an eternity, I obliged her.

"We've never had such an interesting and educational evening," said the woman guest looking at me with soft eyes. I felt empty inside and knew that I had no more kittens waiting to be born. At this point, I was very preoccupied, cleaning and licking my new family. Suddenly, I felt very tired. As the clock chimed ten, Henry lifted my three kittens into the box. I gazed in at my newborns and my heart filled with pride. Then Henry gently picked me up and put me in the box beside them. I snuggled down with my three beautiful kittens and I pulled them close around me with my front paws.

"Well, it's been a very exciting night. We'll leave now and let you get ready for bed," said the male guest.

"Oh, yes, it is getting late," said his wife, and Henry helped them with their coats.

With smiling faces, they headed out the door. Henry and Beth called goodnight to them and I heard the front door close.

"I wonder what we should name them?" Beth asked Henry.

"Oh, let's not think of that for now. I'm tired. Let's go to bed," he answered. Just then, his mouth opened wide and a strange long sound came out.

The house became quiet and the clock chimed eleven times. My three new babies cuddled close to me and began to suckle. Just before the clock chimed midnight, the light went on upstairs and I heard Beth say,

"This is still Ash Wednesday. Let's name them Ashley, Dusty, and Smog."

"That sounds fine," said Henry in a sleepy voice.

In the morning Abner came up from the cellar and came over to our box to visit us right away. He looked at our little three-kitten family and seemed very pleased. As our kittens grew fast, he played with them often and let them jump all over him. Sometimes, he'd have one of their heads in his mouth and he'd growl and pretend to be a fierce lion in Africa. We had our kittens with us for ten weeks. By then, they were hardy and into all kinds of mischief like pouncing on feet, playing hide-and-go-seek in the ashes of the fireplace, knocking over plants, climbing into the grocery bags, and jumping on top of the gramophone records when they were spinning around.

"I've found your beautiful babies very good homes," said Beth to Abner and me one morning. Of course, we felt sad to see our kittens go. But in a way, I was glad as well, as I never had a minute to myself. After that, we were taken to the doctor's office. I was spayed and Abner was neutered. We remained loving companions all the years we lived together in the tall, narrow brick house. Of course, we always remembered Ashley, Dusty and Smog, but we were relieved and happy that they had found wonderful homes.

Then suddenly, I began to feel poorly and after many tests, the doctor said I had diabetes. When I was still a young cat just five years old, The Great Cat in the Sky came and took me to live with him

****

A SNOWY NIGHT

By Blackcat

In Residence: 1982 - 1988

One winter day, when it got dark, Mama picked me up, ran up some stairs, and left me on the foot mat outside a tall, narrow brick house on Pearl Street. I curled into a ball to keep myself warm, but I was very hungry and cold. As it got colder and colder, I prayed that the Great Cat in the Sky would come and take me to live with him. Then the porch light went on, and the door opened. A short man with a little fringe of gray-reddish hair around his head stood in the light and looked up at the sky. He also looked up and down the street and muttered to himself, "Just as I thought, all the cars are buried; and the snow is still falling."

I gave the loudest meow I could, hoping he'd look down and see me. When I meowed again, the man with a kind, cherubic face bent down, picked me up in his warm hand, and brought me inside the cozy house. He held me gently and talked to me. Then he called up the stairs.

"Beth, please come down right away and bring an eyedropper from the medicine cabinet!" A woman with a kind face and brown eyes raced down the stairs. She gazed at me while the man told her that he just went to look outside and then he found me curled up on the foot mat.

"Oh, Henry, what a tiny, black kitten! I'll warm up a fluffy towel in the dryer," she said.

Henry rubbed me dry with a soft yellow duster. Beth heated some milk and poured it into a dish, and with the aid of the eyedropper, the two of them took turns feeding me.

"I'll go and get an empty shoe box and we'll line it with warm towels to make him a little bed," said Henry, handing me to Beth.

"Let's name him Midnight," suggested Beth to him when he returned.

"Since he's all black, how about Blackcat?" offered Henry, caressing my downy coat. "That's a perfect name," agreed Beth. Blackcat is what I was named that very evening. They both tucked me into my little box and put it beside a radiator and the two of them said good night to me. But Henry's face looked worried.

"If you live through the night, I'll see that you get a checkup in the morning," he said, looking down at me. I began to feel warm and I fell into a deep sleep. For the first time that I could remember, I had a full tummy and I was safe and dry.

When I opened my eyes in the morning, I looked up and saw Henry's face. He knelt on the floor next to my box and gently stroked me. Breakfast was more warm milk, this time from a saucer placed on the floor.

I felt afraid and I shivered when they wrapped me in more warm towels and Beth carried me to the car. Henry drove us to the place where a doctor gives checkups to cats and dogs. I lay on a cold table and a cold shiny object, which was attached to the man's ears, was put on my chest. This man wore a white coat and poked me gently here and there. He gave me three quick jabs with a short, sharp thing.

"There now," he said to the couple who named me Blackcat. "He's about five to six weeks old. He was probably born outside. However, by a miracle he's strong and healthy."

He went on to tell them that in a good home, I would grow up to be a fine cat. He also said to bring me back to be neutered – whatever that was - before I was six months old. Going to the doctor's was a regular activity all of my life and I got used to it.

I was a bit on the shy side and spent my time mostly under the footstool in the library, until I became too big to fit under it. Then I found plenty of soft beds upstairs. In warm weather, I lolled in the sun in the courtyard garden. Then when I was about six years old, I became ill and was in a nursing home for a while. The Great Cat in the Sky did come for me early and relieved me of the pain of cancer. But during my life with Beth and Henry, I was happy and content with the good home they gave me. I often think of my caring Mama and how smart she was to have put me on the foot mat outside the tall, narrow brick house on Pearl Street that snowy night in Buffalo, a long time ago.

****

AUNT MARY'S FAVORITE DESSERT

By Queenie Cat

In Residence: 1980 - 1997

U ntil a miracle happened, my life had been miserable in a halfway house for teenage boys who had been in trouble with the law. The boys called me Queenie. "Here! Catch Queenie! Let's score a goal for the Queen City of Buffalo!" the boys would shout and then they'd throw me through the air. Some days I'd have no food or clean water. My litter box was cleaned only once in a while. The fur of my multi-colored gray coat was very long. Most of it was matted and tangled. I fear my days would have been numbered but for a young social worker that came to the institution several times a week. She took a liking to me and said she was worried that I was not being cared for properly.

"Some friends of mine have lost a dear cat recently," she said to me one day. "I think they are looking for another cat to share their home. I'm going to tell them about you." She smiled and stroked me. "You're just a bag of bones under that long coat," she said sadly.

Within a few days, her friends, Beth and Henry came to visit me. After some conversation with the director, they put me into a cat carrier and off I went to live in their tall, narrow brick house.

The first thing they did frightened me a great deal. Beth put me in something called a bathtub! The water made my long hair and my tail plumes look just awful.

"Don't worry," said Beth, drying me with a towel. As she brushed me, she had to cut some tangles out.

"You'll be lovely and fluffy in no time," she said, and she was right.

This new home was a lovely place to be. There was an abundance of seafood and a courtyard with high brick walls where I stretched out and sunbathed, or took a long nap in the shade.

A few weeks after my arrival, Beth said she and Henry were going to give a party for Beth's Aunt Mary who was going to be 90 years old.

"Her favorite dessert is Baked Alaska," said Beth.

I watched her as she separated the yellow from the inside of several eggs. I saw a small blob of yellow fall into the bowl. She added sugar and beat the mixture into little peaks.

"The meringue is not as stiff as it's supposed to be," she said to Henry, looking a bit worried. He got out the block of Neapolitan ice cream from the freezer, took it out of its box and put it on a flat wood board.

'It's hard as a rock," Henry said as he watched Beth covered it over with the meringue.

"How hot do you want the oven?"

"The cookbook says 500 degrees."

"Five hundred degrees! It's amazing that the ice cream doesn't melt!"

"It's only for three minutes, until it browns," Beth assured him.

She put the Baked Alaska on the flat wood board in the hot oven.

The guests went out into the courtyard garden where dessert was to be served. When Beth went back in the kitchen, I followed her. Bubbling, white foam was pouring through the bottom of the oven door and making little rivers and odd-shaped designs on the kitchen floor.

"Oh no!' cried Beth with a shocked look on her face. "The Baked Alaska has melted! I'd a feeling the egg white peaks were too soft!"

Henry grabbed paper towels and began to mop up the floor. I walked over, sat down, and began to lap up the thick creamy stuff. The lovely pink and brown stripes that were in the block of ice cream had disappeared, and it all looked like ivory. The tips of my long fur coat dipped into it and became sticky. My paws were stuck in the gooey, wonderful tasting stuff and Henry had to tug me out of it. Beth said she'd deliver the bad news to the guests. She stood at the kitchen door overlooking the garden.

"Hear ye! Hear ye!" she shouted, cupping her mouth with her hands. The guests in the courtyard became quiet.

"We've had a bit of a disaster. The baked Alaska… melted in the oven!" There was silence for a moment. Then the guests, led by Aunt Mary began to file back into the kitchen.

Aunt Mary took in the scene and she started to laugh. The other guests began to laugh too and they all laughed for a long time.

"Just put it in bowls! It will still taste delicious!" Aunt Mary ordered.

That's what Beth and Henry did. Then everyone sang Happy Birthday and enjoyed eating the melted Baked Alaska. Aunt Mary said it was one of the best parties she ever had.

When everyone went home, Henry and I ate the last of the dessert. Then as the clock chimed ten times, to my horror, he said,

"And now Queenie, my young lady with your long sticky coat, and your sugary plumed tail, you must... have a bath."

He reached for my bathtub and filled it with warm, sudsy water. If you remember, I just hated to have baths.

****

A VALENTINE'S DAY CONFESSION

By Queenie Cat

In Residence: 1980 – 1997

Valentine's Day   Buffalo, New York

My Dear Mrs. Reggie,

This Valentine's Day I need to pour out my heart to you, my esteemed consultant and dear friend. Two big events have occurred in my life. One is that dear, gentle Blackcat who had been in a nursing home for three months, died on Monday. He had been feeling poorly because of cancer. While he was a loyal companion, and I miss him, I'm glad he did not have to suffer any longer.

Beth often talks about you and your longtime friendship. She says your husband tells her a letter from me to you makes you smile while you go through your own cancer treatment.

The second event, which I report with a mix of joy and chagrin, is that I have fallen … hopelessly in love. I'm a bit embarrassed about it really. I don't know what people would say about me if they knew I had become involved with this person. This man walks in the door at nine in the morning, five days a week. But because of his station in life, he is not at all a suitable companion for me. Still, I sit in the kitchen and listen for his footsteps, my eyes riveted on the door, waiting for him. You see dear friend … I have lost my heart to a … stripper! I can hear you say,

"Oh, how unlike Queenie. How unsuitable!" you will say. But I cannot help myself, and feel entirely out of control.

As soon as this man enters, the first thing he does is spread a thick cloth on the table. I jump up on it and roll over on my back. My eyes beg him to take me in his arms. He makes a big fuss over me. What makes it worse is I can tell by his smell that he has other felines in his life. Nevertheless, I lie on the table all day watching him use a heat gun and putty knife to remove paint from the wainscoting and cabinets in the kitchen. Time stands still while I follow his every move. While I am getting on in years, I have to admit this is my first ever love affair. It's so glorious that it boggles my mind as well as every atom and fiber of my being.

As my dear friend for many years, I want you to know that this big love has come into my life. I am not asking for your advice. I don't want any well-meaning opinions. I just want to be held in my stripper's arms forever!

Your friend, Queenie

P.S. I hope you will continue to be my dear friend.

****

SMOKE GOT IN MY EYES

By Queenie Cat

In Residence: 1980 -1997

"Queenie Cat, Henry and I are having six friends over for dinner," Beth told me. I watched her while she pulled treasures of the sea out of white wrappings. She washed them and placed them in crystal bowls. I loved it when we had company. I'd spend much time grooming myself and I was delighted that my fluffy tail had ballooned out to perfection. Visitors always admired me and said my tall tail was my best attribute.

"We're having shrimp as a first course," Beth said as my eyes followed her every move from my chair in the kitchen. I jumped down and followed her into the dining room.

"I gave you a taste of shrimp earlier today," she reminded me as she lit two tall green candles on the table and dimmed the lights in the ceiling. Sure, one little shrimp, but surely I'll get more, I thought to myself. The candles gave the room a soft, warm glow and made the crystal and Beth's silver hair gleam. She lit two more green candles and placed them beside the china plates and silver forks at the end of the buffet. The candlelight made the mahogany wood shine. When she went back into the kitchen, I jumped up and sat on one end of the buffet so I could watch everything better. Beth returned and surveyed the table. From the soft look in her brown eyes, I knew everything was just the way she wanted it to be.

After the guests enjoyed cocktails, they sat at the table for dinner.

"This is the most delicious shrimp I've ever had," a gentleman said.

It was true that earlier in the afternoon I'd sampled the delicious jumbo shrimp. But while I watched him eat the fat, pink shrimp, I couldn't stop licking my lips. There was much talk and laughter. It was clear they had forgotten about me. Then a succulent roast beef was carried out on a platter. All eyes were on Henry while he carved it into thick slices.

No one looked over at me. Being ignored was the hardest thing for me to accept. To get some attention, I started my usual little trick of flicking my tail from side to side. I gently flipped it and then I flopped it. There was no reaction so I did it faster. Still, there was no attention. This was hard for me to take. Swish that tail faster, I said to myself. Faster, Queenie Cat! Hey, wait a minute. Stop! I smelled something smoking. Maybe Beth left something burning in the oven. Suddenly the guest who was raving about the shrimp, dropped his fork on his china plate, and jumped up from his chair. His eyes seemed too big for his face. He pointed at me and in a voice that made me nervous he cried, "Look! Queenie Cat's on fire!"

Now everyone looked in my direction. More forks and knives clattered onto plates. Henry jumped up. He grabbed my beautiful, fat plumed tail and ran his hand from the bottom to the top and back again. Smoke got in my eyes.

"I thought I smelled something burning!" he said. He then grabbed me and put me under his arm and brought me down to the cellar. He got a damp towel and washed my tail.

"You're OK now," he said, "only a few plumes missing." He walked up the stairs and closed the door. I began to clean my tail. Ugh! It tasted awful. Now, not only was my tail grabbed in an undignified fashion in front of guests and strangers, I was escorted from the dining room, brought to the cellar and now I'm banished from the dinner party. What went wrong here? Surely, there must be some mistake. I meowed and got no answer. I meowed louder and louder. Finally I heard footsteps coming down the stairs. It was Henry again. He was carrying a plate with a little of the roast beef I'd been watching before all this crazy commotion started.

"Everything will be alright," he said, "but you have to stay down here until our guests leave." He told me not to worry.

"Your plumes just got singed a bit. Your best attribute will grow back and balloon out thick and fluffy soon again," he assured me.

****

THE POSTMAN BRINGS

A SPECIAL PACKAGE

By Queenie Cat

In Residence: 1980 - 1997

Beth and her friend Mary worked in the health care field. They also owned a small mail order publishing firm known as Potentials Development that printed educational information on how to help people who were growing old to keep active, well and happy. They sent their mailings to directors who organized physical activities in nursing homes. Beth decided to write and include a two-page newsletter called "Feline Fine Mews" in outgoing packages, with the hope that people in nursing homes, who enjoyed cats, would find it entertaining. One newsletter announced that personal stories about cats were wanted and a prize would be given for the best entry.

A lady named Margaret, who lived in a nursing home in California, read the newsletter and submitted a story about her male cat named 'Dirty Nose.' Her story won the prize, and a stuffed cat with a collar and tag, with her cat's name on it, were sent to her. The letter announcing that she had won the grand prize was signed with my name, Queenie Cat. Margaret wrote me a lovely thank you note. Then she wrote again to say she was sending me a gift she had bought when she went on a trip to a shopping mall in the nursing home van. In her letter she said it was the first time in over a year that she had gone out anywhere. She told me to expect the gift in the mail soon.

Indeed the gift, addressed to me, arrived shortly: a pair of salt and peppershakers in the shape of two handsome cats. I was touched and delighted. I sent Margaret a warm thank you note and we began to send letters to each other on a regular basis, even exchanging some small gifts from time to time. Margaret wrote that she now even enjoyed going to the shopping center in the van provided by the nursing home.

About a year after Margaret had won the contest for the best cat story, Beth went on a business trip to California. She spent a weekend in the city where Margaret lived, and went to visit her. Beth told me that at that time, people could not have cats in nursing homes and that some old people there were very lonely. Margaret and I continued to write letters back and forth. Quite some time passed. I was aware no letter had come from Margaret in several weeks, and I became worried. Beth said that she would phone the nursing home to inquire about her.

One morning as I was taking my bath, the doorbell rang. Beth opened it and saw the postman standing there holding a package.

"This is for Queenie, and she has to sign for it," he said.

"Queenie is unavailable at the moment. I'll sign it for her," Beth replied and brought in the package. I watched as she carefully opened the box that had a California postmark. She picked out an envelope and opened it. As she read the letter, her face grew sad. She sat down and told me it was bad news. Then, she read the letter out loud to me.

'Dear Queenie Cat,

I regret to inform you that our dear Margaret has died. Your letters and gifts were a source of great joy and comfort to her. With the exception of her television and radio, she has left her entire estate to you, Queenie Cat. Her estate is enclosed in this box.'

"It's signed by the secretary of Margaret's nursing home," Beth told me and her eyes were misty.

Beth opened the package and found a shirt with a cat's picture on the front that I had sent to Margaret some time ago. Another package contained two beautiful china cats with flowers around their necks. Now, there were tears in Beth's eyes as she placed them on a high shelf in the library for all to admire. That's where you will find my treasured inheritance to this very day.

****

MY BIG BIRTHDAY BASH

By Abner O'Grady

In Residence: 1967 - 1988

For days, I watched Beth and Henry design yellow and black invitations. Then they put them in yellow envelopes and mailed them out to 60 friends and family members inviting them to my important twentieth birthday party.

'Admission is by presentation of a picture, poem, song, or other printed material relevant to the ancient world of felines,' the invitation said. Beth spent days cooking dishes that gave the whole house the smell of the sea.

"It's time to get dressed for the party," she said when the big day arrived. Queenie, Blackcat and I gazed at Beth. She looked lovely in a black dress and her hair shone like silver. She placed a splendid orange ribbon decorated with fresh forsythia around Queenie's collar. She put a handsome green, red and orange plaid ribbon around Blackcat's neck.

And Henry arranged a gilded, heavy, azure-blue ribbon around my neck so it hung down on my chest.

"It certainly dresses up a gray tabby like you," Henry said to me, his eyes dancing. People began to arrive in small groups, many of the women wore earrings, necklaces, belts, and carried fancy purses. Some dresses, shirts and ties sported beautiful feline designs.

Blackcat escaped out into the courtyard garden and his sleek black coat stayed well hidden under the hedges that were a vibrant green that spring night in May. All he showed were the slits of his bright green eyes. I slinked in and out of the garden and tried to persuade him to come in and join in my birthday bash. But he said no. He told me the last time there was a party, a woman with spiked heels jabbed one down on his paw. He shrieked in such a high voice that she dropped her glass and crystal scattered all over the floor.

"This always happens to me when I rub against women's shins at cocktail parties," he told me.

Queenie Cat was her gracious and self-important self. As usual, she was so much in the limelight many guests thought the birthday party was for her. Because I was the birthday boy, however, some people offered me jumbo shrimp from their party plates. I was polite and ate everything I was offered.

The magic moment that memorable spring night came when Henry went into the living room and sat at the piano. He asked for everyone's attention. The living room was full of people, and the crowd overflowed into the library. Henry began to play:

"Happy Birthday Dear Abner," Everybody sang the words and they all looked so silly. There was clapping and cheering and the guests raised their glasses to me. Then someone brought out a chocolate cake decorated with yellow and blue icing with 20 candles flaming on the top. My name was written in chocolate. The guests sang, "How old are you?" I thought that was silliest song of all because my age was on the invitation. They all knew right well that this was my 20th birthday. Everyone had a piece of my chocolate cake and they raved about how delicious it was. Henry ate a blue piece that said 'Abner' on it. He went back to the piano again and played more songs. People sang:

"For He's A Jolly Good Fellow" to me, and Henry's face beamed. Then he read a proclamation saying it was Cat Day in Erie County, in the majestic, Empire State of New York. The guests cheered and clapped again. I was so proud and happy. I was the Cat of the Day. Henry played other songs as well, including my favorite, "Alley Cat." Guests read short stories and recited poems. A few people told stories about their own cats and they made many people laugh. It was a unique, literary evening for sure.

I high stepped on the coffee table full of gifts for me. Presents were stacked all over the floor as well. When the church bell rang eight times, Beth led the guests into the living room and sat in a big armchair. She cradled me in the well of her lap and opened my presents, which were wrapped in all kinds of fancy paper with colorful bows. My eyes were as big as moons. Cameras flashed when I saw the cans of Clams Chez Louis, Ocean Perch, Canadian Salmon, Maine Oysters, Dublin Bay Prawns, and Alaskan Crab. A strange-shaped package with a smell of mint turned out to be a live catnip plant. There were small packets of my favorite brand of catnip as well. Women O o oh ed and men Aa ah ed when their eyes landed on my new dinner bowl filled to the brim with shrimp puffs. A jazzy leather collar and fluffy red blanket brought more raves and gasps. There was even a practical present of a giant bag of cat litter. I received a snazzy six-pack of the brand-new odor-free 'Litter Fresh," and a letter from a major corporation.

"Be careful! That Litter Fresh made my cat forget where his litter box was," said a woman guest with a big voice.

When the guests were leaving, Henry gave each one a souvenir of a yellow flag with a silhouette of a black cat on it. When he closed the door after the last guest had left, Beth removed Queenie's collar. Queenie yawned and without even a glance to me, the birthday boy, she went up the front staircase. I knew she'd be asleep in no time in her favorite chair in the guest bedroom. She always made sure to get her beauty rest.

Beth and Henry said they were tired and would leave the washing up until the morning. They called Blackcat to come in from the garden. They said good night to us and went up the stairs after Queenie. Soon, the house was quiet. Blackcat and I went into the kitchen. We quietly got into the garbage can where we found some left over jumbo shrimp and gobbled it up. We finished off a fish-shaped container of salmon mousse as well. Blackcat teased me about how silly I looked with my chain on my chest. I pawed it off over my head. I asked him did he have any idea how he looked in the green, red and orange plaid ribbon? He pawed his ribbon off too. We swished our tails and stared into each other's eyes.

Then we lunged at each other and started to wrestle. He was only five years old, but old as I was, I still have broad shoulders and could hold my own with him. We knocked into the strange packet that smelled of mint. We bit it and tore it open. It spilled all over the floor. We sniffed it, rolled in it, and we ate it. We felt so happy it's just impossible to describe. We chased each other up and down the five staircases in the house. We crashed into the presents. We had one good boxing match. We wrestled on the floor again and our coats became covered in beautiful catnip.

I lay on my back looking out at the starry night through the lace curtains. The sky turned from navy to blood red. Then pearly puffs began to appear and cascade down. Birds started to chirp in their nests at the top of the ivied walls around the courtyard garden. The clock chimed five times, and all of a sudden, I felt very drowsy. I could barely jump up on the living room couch. Blackcat jumped into a soft armchair. I fell fast asleep. I dreamed of mountains of Alaskan Crab floating on mounds of ice... rivers of Canadian Salmon ... that's the last I remember of my big birthday bash.

****

A POST SCRIPT FROM QUEENIE

The year 1988 was the best of times and the worst of times. Blackcat and Abner both went up to the Great Cat in the Sky. I was appointed to the position of historian and recording secretary.

Sadly, dear, kind Henry died in 1989. Beth was alone and I was the only cat in the house. For a while, we were sad and lonely. Still, I rather liked having Beth all to myself, just the two of us. We had wonderful times together. Then as I became older, I began to feel poorly and the doctor shook his head and said there was nothing more he could do for me. In 1997, I joined the other cats with the Great Cat in the Sky. But just before I left,

I listened in on Beth's nightly phone conversations and I heard her talking to a woman in California. I was relieved and happy to hear that more cats were going to come and live in our tall, narrow brick house.

****

FROM A HOME IN THE SUN TO

A HOME IN THE SNOW

By MONIQUE

In Residence: 1997 - Still Living

"California girl, well-traveled, exotic French name" was how Stacy, the woman who took me into her home, described me. Isaac had been living with her only a few weeks when I arrived. He was always in his own little world, but he and I became silent friends. Stacy often talked on the phone to a man in a faraway place called Buffalo. One night her eyes lit up with happiness.

"He's asked me to marry him," she told Isaac and me. "We're all going to live in Buffalo!"

Days before we left California, Stacy found out that her future husband was allergic to felines.

She called a woman named Beth and told her the situation. Soon after that phone call, we headed for Buffalo. After three nights in motels, we arrived at the tall, narrow brick house on Pearl Street. Beth had our beds ready and gave us all the shrimp puffs we could eat.

Before I found a home with Stacy, my life had been unbearable and I ran away from the house where I was born. While I though I looked beautiful in my sleek, all-black coat, the residents of the house thought cats that were all black were bad omens. Every time I appeared, they kicked me and screamed at me. I ran and hid under the furniture to get away from them. The experience left me nervous, and I'd no confidence or social skills at all. In my Buffalo home, I had every luxury. Soft chairs and feather beds of my choice were always available for catnaps. Clocks chimed while I stretched in front of the glowing fire. A variety of river and ocean fish was often on the menu. I was brushed and combed and taken to my own doctor. There was a beautiful outdoor courtyard for sunbathing. It was full of shady trees and fresh catnip in the warm months. I hoped I'd found the home I'd always been yearning to find. However, that was not to be my good fortune.

I've had a fear of outdoor noises for as long as I can remember. Probably from being treated badly in my early life, I'm still jumpy and nervous. In fact, the first time I ventured into the courtyard garden in the new house, a leaf fell from the lilac tree and the wind rustled it along the patio. When I heard it, I was so terrified I fled inside and hid under the bed. It was ages before I had the courage to venture out again. Most of the hours of my days were spent in an armchair in Beth's bedroom. She always stroked me gently as she came and went from that room and she also talked to me, inviting me to come downstairs or into the garden. But mostly, except to go to my litter box, I turned my head away and remained in that chair. One day, Beth said,

"I'm going away to hospital for two weeks. Someone will come and take care of you each day."

I'd no idea I'd miss her so much. Isaac and I were the only two cats in the house, and while people did come and take care of us, we were very lonely and afraid. The night Beth came back home, I jumped on her lap, and purred and purred. Her brown eyes were so happy and misty; I stayed buried in her soft lap for over an hour.

Soon after, a friend of Beth's came to stay for a while. One snowy night she and Beth went out with the cat carrier. They brought home a feline that had always lived on the streets. She had a high screeching voice. She was bossy and flashed her claws and her canines at me whenever I came downstairs or passed her in the hall. A few times Isaac arched his back and hissed and spat in an effort to protect me. Beth noticed my fear and that I'd also lost my appetite. She called her friend, Betty and said,

"Betty, the street cat is too much for poor Monique. She's not faring well with this streetwise, afraid-of-nothing female."

Betty, who often came to help Beth keep the house sparkling and always had cat treats in her pocket, said,

"I'd love to have Monique come and live with me."

She came for me right away and off I went to the quiet home where I am one of four gentle cats and I'm so serene and happy. I hope I won't ever have to leave or travel again. I often think of dear Isaac with great fondness. I know that he prefers to be alone and I wonder how he copes being with the other cats in the tall, narrow brick house. I won't say more about him now. I'll let him tell his own story. Still, I wonder if he ever thinks of our old California days. I wonder if he sometimes remembers me...his old friend Monique.

****

MY LITTLE WORLD

By Isaac Guardian

In Residence: 1997 – Present

I was only a few months old when I found myself in my first good home in California. Soon after I'd settled in, shy Monique with the beautiful, black velvet coat joined us. (My own dark gray tabby coat would not make me stand out in a crowd.) Neither of us could remember anything about being kittens. She was the only one with an inner understanding that I preferred to be by myself and that I was happiest of all when I was off in my own little world.

We heard rumors that we were going to go all across the country to Buffalo, New York. One day Monique and I were packed into separate little prison cells and put on the back seat of a car. We drove and drove during the day and stayed in hotels at night. Finally, we arrived in Buffalo. We arrived at the wide oak door of a tall, narrow brick house. Beth, the woman who lived there, really loved felines. She opened the door and greeted us warmly. There were no other cats living there when we arrived, but that all changed over time.

I don't know when it started, but as long as I can remember, I've been nervous and frightened when men are anywhere around. To let them know to keep their distance, I arched my gray back, made my tail big and fluffy, and I hissed and spat at them. I showed them my canines as well. I did not even trust Jim, who works for Beth taking care of the flower garden. He is kind and he does love cats. He was *very* patient with me, and he did everything to please me, but still I'd hiss and spit at him.

I made a huge fuss whenever Jim tried to put me into the dreaded cat prison and take me to the doctor, who also was a man. I attempted to escape and ran pell mell up and down the five staircases in the house. My fat belly would hit each step of the stairs and slow me down. Still, it took Jim about an hour to catch me as he chased after me with a blanket in his hands. As I got tired, I felt the blanket billow over me and I could not see anything at all. I was so afraid of the dark and I felt I could not breathe. All I could do was lie very still. Then Jim shoved me into the cat prison, which had a very confined space, but I could look out.

Once at the doctor's office, I was terrified of the huge barking dogs. I had no control at all. All I could do was be very quiet and pretend I was not there. Then the doctor subjected me to all kinds of probing and jabs that hurt. When at last Jim brought me home, I'd disappear upstairs and hide there for a day. I've become better about going to the doctor, but I still try to avoid it and run up and down the stairs when I see the cat carrier.

One winter night it was snowing hard and Beth went out with the cat carrier and brought home another cat that lived down the street. The new cat was real bossy and mean to Monique. Sometimes Monique would be so afraid, I'd hunch up my back and make my gray fur and tail look bigger in an effort to protect her. Suddenly one day, Monique went off in another cat carrier. I never saw her again. In a way, I was glad I didn't have to take care of her. But I often wonder how she fared when she went to live with the woman who comes to help Beth keep the house nice and shiny. Monique was the only one that did not put demands on me to socialize. She understood I was happiest of all when I was just by myself.

My chief activity for years has been to drag bright colored pieces of ribbon and yarns down one staircase and up another one.

"There he goes," Jim, the man who tends the garden says. "Isaac's goin' huntin' again."

I pretend to be an explorer and I discover exotic materials. Other times, I go on safari and I bring back a small stuffed giraffe or a dog. I have fun by myself when I carry or bat them up and down the stairs.

"Isaac, you've been on Safari again. You are a great hunter indeed! Thanks for the trophies!" Beth often says. Then I go off by myself again.

If I could have my way, I'd be happy living as the only cat in the house. Lately I heard Beth and Jim talking in the kitchen.

"Isaac doesn't hiss or spit at me any more," said Jim.

"Yes," said Beth. "I've noticed. After all of these years, he's learned to trust and be a bit affectionate too."

At night, I wait at the top of the stairs for Beth and I follow her into her bedroom. She closes the door, sits in her chair and takes off her makeup. While she brushes her silver hair, I purr in her lap. Then she gets into bed and reads a few chapters of a book. When she puts out the light, I jump off the bed. In no time at all, I find just the right spot on the rug on the floor at the end of her bed. I fall asleep on my back with my four legs bent at the knees, and my paws curled under.

****

COUNTRY BOY MOVES TO THE CITY

By Jacob Picasso

In Residence: 2000 to Present

At about five months old, I was tossed from a car window and flew through the air before landing on my feet in a farmer's field. For hours, I lay low in the grass getting over the shock of it. Then, as night came, I crawled through the tall grass and made my way into the barn where I found a tender mouse for my dinner.

"I need a good mouser in the house!" said the farm owner one day, when she saw me catch a mouse.

"Come on into my farm house!" I met her expectations and caught her many plump field mice. We cuddled together and watched television at night. She became very fond of me and I was happy with her. But one day, she picked up the phone and her voice was sad.

"Is this the St. Francis Rescue Society?" she asked, her voice quivering.

A man's deep voice answered, "Yes."

"I've a short-haired American domestic male cat. He's gorgeous, wearing a marmalade-colored fur coat trimmed in scarves of thick ermine. He's a champion mouser. But I have to find him a new home because I'm selling the farm," and her eyes welled up.

The next day a man came and knocked at the door. In his hand was a prison cell my size. The woman of the house cried as he put me into it. He told her not to worry, because a handsome dude like me would find a good home in no time.

He took me to the St. Francis Rescue Society where the doctor examined me and said I was healthy. He put me to sleep and did an operation. When I woke up he said,

"Sorry, dude, you'll never be a Papa."

I had my own compartment and people came to look at me. The woman who sold her farm came to visit me as well. One day a staff person said to her,

"I'm taking him to visit a woman who lives in the City of Buffalo. She loves St. Francis."

The helper from St. Francis and the woman who sold the farm packed me into the prison cell again and put me in a car. After over an hour, the car stopped on a narrow shady street in front of a tall, narrow brick house. The woman from St. Francis rapped the brass doorknocker. When the door opened, I saw a brown-eyed woman who looked very kind. She said her name was Beth. She invited us in and with a big smile she said,

"Please open his carrier door."

I jumped out and started my explorations. Loud spits and hisses came from a male cat as he crouched behind the leg of an antique table. In the spirit of goodwill and fellowship, I gently touched his nose with my paw and proceeded to explore my surroundings. In the dining room, I met a female cat that arched her back and showed me her canines. However, I coolly walked around, even though I noticed that the cats in residence had joined forces to protest my presence. When Beth invited me to jump into her lap, I sailed through the air and landed right there. That seemed the right thing to do because papers were signed right after that. Then Beth said,

"Everything will calm down in a while. I'm going to call you Jacob." Then she picked me up and carried me through all the rooms of the tall, narrow brick house.

****

THE VISITOR WHO DID NOT LIKE CATS

By Jacob Picasso

In Residence : 2000 - Present

On a beautiful midday in early August, Beth said she was inviting a new friend named Ruth over for lunch. I watched her as she spent the morning making a dish in the shape of a fish. She carried her good china outside to the garden.

"We'll have lunch out in the courtyard today," she said. " Ruth will enjoy the water lilies which are in full bloom just now."

Just as the nearby church bells rang noon, there was a knock on the door. I looked at the other cats and we walked into the living room so we could get a look at this new visitor. We stood together while Beth opened the door wide.

"Ruth, how lovely to see you. Come on in," Beth greeted the trim woman holding a bouquet of wildflowers.

"I'm delighted to be here," said the woman with short, curly silver hair. Then her eyes looked over Beth's shoulder and landed on us.

"Oh, my goodness!" said the visitor. "I didn't know you had cats!"

"Yes, I do," Beth answered and she told her our names.

"Oh, dear," Ruth said, "I don't feel comfortable around cats at all!"

"I'm sorry to hear that," said Beth. "It's no problem at all. I'll put them all down in the cellar." She scooped us up and did just that. We just hated it when we were put in the cellar. It deprived us of using our persuasive charms and powers on new people. From the window ledge in the cellar, we could heard them talking and watch them eating. Butterflies yo-yoed over the colorful flowers, and birds sang at the top of the tall ivied walls.

"I play golf in all the spare time I have," I heard Ruth telling Beth.

"It's great exercise and a wonderful way to keep fit," Beth replied.

After they had eaten their dessert, Beth came down to the cellar to tell us we were being good and she gave us some treats. Just then, the phone rang and she ran up the stairs to answer it. She forgot to close the cellar door. I slipped up the stairs and hid in the pantry. She then left the door to the courtyard open for a minute while she carried used dishes back into the kitchen. This was the moment I'd been waiting for.

I slipped out into the courtyard and hid in the flowers. Eying Ruth, I got myself ready. Then I sprang through the air and plop: there I was right in the center of Ruth's trim lap. She looked startled for a moment. Just then Beth came out, saw me and came over to pick me up. However, Ruth had begun to stroke me ever so gently and I purred in response. She looked up at Beth with smiling eyes and said,

"Well, he's a bold one! Oh! Beth, let Jacob stay in my lap."

I was pleased with myself that I'd won her over. I settled down and was on my very best behavior. I knew all that I needed was a little time to use my charm and persuasive powers. That's why I always look forward to the times when Beth invites new friends to come and visit.

"Could you come over the same day next week to have dinner and to meet Betty, a friend who is in my book club?" offered Beth as Ruth was leaving.

"That would be lovely," Ruth answered.

When the week passed and the church bell rang six times, the doorbell also rang once. Beth opened the door. There was Ruth holding another bouquet of flowers.

Minutes later, the bell rang again and there was Betty with a plant and a book in her hands. She always made a fuss over me and I loved the smell of her cats.

Ruth looked at us and her face had a soft, lovely look. I was so happy to see her, my heart started to beat fast. Before Betty and Ruth arrived, Beth had given us the usual lecture to be nice cats and not bother the guests. At the last minute, however, Beth decided to put us in the cellar. I was so disappointed at being banished from the dinner. But after dessert was served, Beth came and opened the door. I rushed into the living room and saw Ruth sitting in the armchair drinking coffee. Betty was on the sofa reading out loud from a book.

I was so happy to see that Ruth was still in the house. Lying on the floor gazing at her, I had an urge to be back in her comforting lap. She lifted the cup of coffee to her mouth. At that moment, I crouched. I sprang. I flew through the air, aiming myself at the center of her lap. However, I missed it by a beat and landed in the Dresden saucer instead. She held on tight to the cup and her face looked worried as the hot coffee splashed all over me. Oh, dear, I noticed there were wet coffee stains on Ruth's dress too.

Beth rushed to the kitchen to get paper towels to clean up the mess. She apologized, but Ruth told her not to worry. Then, everything calmed down and Beth, Ruth and Betty retired to the library. It was now Ruth's turn to read. While she held the book up near her face, I crouched. I sprang. I sailed through the air. Bingo. I landed in the center of her lap. Ruth began to stroke me right away and I settled down.

"Jacob," she said, "You make me feel so special. After all the years I thought I did not like cats, I really do love you." She kept on reading and I stayed in her lap with my purr on low.

****

A Thank You Letter

Feline Fine Mews
Pearl St.
Buffalo, NY 14202

MRS R. ASTMANN
30 EREHWON ST.
BUFFALO NY 14200

By Jacob Picasso

In Residence : 2000 - Present

D ear Miss Ruth,

The purpose of this letter is to thank you for all you did for me yesterday. Nobody ever, ever before got down on their backside and spun around like a top on our kitchen floor! What a treat to watch you in action. You have kept very active. I'm wondering if it is because you are a great walker and you play so much golf?

It was too bad that the ball you brought me as a present went under the stove at first throw. You and I never got a chance to play with it together, which makes me sad. Perhaps you will bring me another ball sometime soon. Beth told me that you are now 88 years old. She is 12 years younger than you but she can't kneel down any more. She tried hard to get the ball out from under the stove, but so far, no luck.

Thank you for letting me take a nap in your lap when you come to visit and for your gift and the demonstration of unforgettable acrobatic skill. With deep appreciation and affection.

Yours truly,

Jacob Picasso, historian and recording secretary

****

A WISH COMES TRUE

By Rachael Louise

In Residence: 2002 To Present

I've no memory of being a baby. Since I was young, I'd been roaming the streets of Buffalo alone. My home was under the porch of a big old house at the end of Pearl Street. An old man and his wife were the only people that lived there. The street is lined with shade trees that in summer make canopies over the tall, narrow brick houses. The bells of a nearby old church never forget to ring the hours.

When the wind from Lake Erie howled and threw blankets of snow over the city, I jumped over deep mounds and peered in through the window at the couple that let me stay under their porch. At first they would ignore me. But after a while,

I'd catch their eyes. Their faces became soft, and they talked to each other. Then the woman walked to the door and she opened it enough for me to squeeze inside and stay in their warm house for the night. They gave me dinner scraps from their table too. I was more than grateful.

But early in the morning, firm hands picked me up and plopped me outside, and the door shut behind me. As my gesture of thanks for the warm night's lodgings, I shook my short, charcoal fur coat and walked off with my orange ringed-tail high in the air.

My first place to go to was the tallest, narrow brick house up the street, where two other cats lived. I went up on the porch and jumped on the window ledge. Through the lace curtains, I saw a cat the color of marmalade stretched out dozing in front of the blazing fire. The other gray cat was in the lap of the lady of the house. She had gentle brown eyes, and a soft kind face, framed by silver hair. Many visitors came to see her and I heard them call her Beth.

One day I noticed a new, sleek, all-black female cat had arrived at the house. I wondered how these cats were so lucky to live in such a warm, cozy place. After years of looking in through windows, my one big wish was to sit on top of a sofa and look out at the snow from inside a warm house.

One spring the old woman who lived in the house over my porch died, and in the fall, the man died too. I stayed under the porch and some kindly neighbors came and left me some cat food. In November, the cruelest of arctic weather came to Buffalo. I was panic-stricken. What would I do now

without the white-haired couple who always let me
in on a bad night? As the snow fell heavily, Beth
trudged through the snow towards me. She had
a neighbor with her. They brought a sturdy box,
padded with soft warm pieces of old blankets and
towels. They also left me cat food that had the
smell of the sea, and fresh water. They did this
every day while the snow enveloped the city.

On my spy visits to the house up the street to see
what the other cats were up to, I saw there was
another woman living in the house now. She didn't
talk much and she never smiled. But one very
cold night soon after she arrived, she came with
Beth to feed me and I heard her say that she and
her husband had two cats.

"Would you take this one to the cat doctor for a
check-up in the morning?" Beth asked her.

"I will. I'll get up early and take her," said the friend, and they walked back up the street. Check-up? What could it be I wondered as I dozed in my box.

Next morning, I was up very early. I felt excited and happy. I washed my face, my ears and my bib. My four paws were spotless. I sat and waited. But the friend did not come. While church bells rang on, I just waited and waited. I began to feel sad. Then I saw her coming towards me, carrying something strange.

"This is a cat carrier," she said, putting me in it. I hissed and showed her my claws.

"Oh, settle down" she ordered. "I'm taking you to the doctor." I did as I was told.

When we arrived at the doctor's office, dogs of all sizes were barking and my heart was beating like a hammer. Soon, I was carried into a small room. Huge hands grabbed me and put me on an ice-cold shiny table. There was a smell that took my breath away. Big lights were put into my eyes. I was poked and prodded all over. I wondered when this terrible experience would be over.

"She's really quite healthy," the doctor said, and he gave me two jabs with a sharp little thing. At that moment, I showed him my long sharp claws. He wrote something on paper and gave it to the woman who brought me there. For the first time, she gave me a beautiful smile. She put me back in the cat carrier and drove me back to my old house.

Back on my porch, she took me out of the carrier and gently placed me back in my box. She covered me with a piece of blanket and said, "Good night." I watched her as she walked back to the house where she now lived with Beth and the three cats. My heart was heavy. I'd hoped the home up the street would be mine after that visit to the doctor. Sadly meowing, I settled down for the night. Not long afterward, I recognized Beth's voice coming down the street. I looked through the heavy swirling snow. All the houses and trees looked like they were bandaged. With her was her friend who had taken me to the doctor. She had the cat carrier in her hand. Oh, no, I don't want to go to the doctor's again! The church bells rang nine times while they lifted me up.

"We're taking you to live with us," said Beth. They wrapped me up and put me back in the cat carrier. I made no fuss at all. We entered the wide oak door of the house on Pearl Street and I was allowed to walk on the lovely red carpet. I roamed the warm house with my tail high in the air, and I was so happy, I didn't go to sleep at all. I stretched in front of the fire and thought wishes do come true. In the morning, Beth looked at me for a long time. "I'm going to call you Rachael Louise," she announced.

As the days went by, I visited the woman with the sad blue eyes who slept most of the day in her bed upstairs. She reached out and stroked me. I purred for her and she drew me in close. One morning, she placed me under her neck and we both went down the stairs where the smell of Canadian bacon was in every corner of the kitchen. Our love affair went on for several days. Then one morning she held me very tight.

"Goodbye. I'm going back home," she said and her blue eyes were happy.

Four years later, I'm the only female cat sharing the tall, narrow brick house with male cats known as "The Boys." Every day when I stride past them, they bow their heads and lower their eyes. Sometimes, just to remind them that indeed, I am the boss, I stop, hiss at them and I stretch out my claws. Then, I walk past them slowly with my eyes in the distance and my tail high in the air.

I watch all the seasons from inside flower-potted windows. In summer, I go out into the courtyard garden. I hide in the ivy, make my eyes into slits, and watch the birds. I copy the tail signals of the squirrels. I sharpen my claws on the trunks of trees.

In winter, I sit on top of the sofa and look out at the snow. Mostly my time indoors is spent in the upstairs studio with Beth. She is involved in many interesting activities. I stretch across her desk with my claws tucked in and she tells me about a new book she is writing. She often tells me that I am good company and that she is happy she rescued me from under the porch down the street, that cold, snowy night. I purr to let her know that I'm more than content. All I have ever wished for was to live with her in the tall, narrow brick house, and she has made my wish come true.

****

BUBBA COMES BACK TO THE NEIGHBORHOOD

By Bubba

In Residence: 2007 - Present

I'm *Bubba*. People call me Big Boy. Moon faced, large boned, with a fur coat the color of marmalade, I now tip the scales at thirty pounds. I'm described as a handsome specimen of a short hair American domestic cat. When I was young, I used to live in the house next door. I loved to sit outside on the small front porch, bask in the sun and watch the world go by. Most of all, I watched the dark-haired man who took care of the garden of the tall, narrow brick house beside mine. His name is Jim. Between weeding, planting, growing and watering beautiful flowers, Jim often came over to me, scratched my ears with his big strong hands and said, "Hey, Big Boy!"

I've been with the gardener for years now. Imagine my surprise that the two of us are back living on Pearl Street in the house beside my original home. The lady named Beth still owns the house and Jim has remained her gardener.

Here's what happened in my life and how I came back home. When I first lived on Pearl Street, I was very happy. But one day, after years of contentment, the lady who first took care of me called Jim aside and said.

"I'm going to move to Florida. I'm looking for a good home for the cat."

"Oh!" said Jim, looking very surprised.

"If I don't find him a home soon, I'll have to put him to sleep," my owner continued, and Jim's eyebrows shot up in horror. My own heart beat like a hammer. Jim came over and scratched my ears.

"Hey, Big Boy! Let me talk this over with my roommate, Mike," he said.

The next day he came back and rapped on our door.

"With your permission, my friend and I would like to take him," he offered gently. My owner looked at me and her face became sad. She gathered up my basket, my bowl, and my kitty litter box. She scooped me up and said,

"Hey, Big Boy, I'm going to miss you." She squeezed me tightly and put me in my cat carrier in the front seat. I looked up and saw her eyes were misty.

"Don't worry. I'll take good care of him," said Jim. I felt sad too and I just stared ahead.

Jim and his friend Mike lived in an apartment about two miles away and later we moved to another one down near the waterfront. However, in neither one did I have outdoor privileges. Suddenly Mike became very sick, and after a month, he died. Jim was shocked and very sad. We had to leave the apartment so the two of us moved to the home of Jim's niece, whose nickname is Penny. Her constant companion was a small dog named Ariel. Since I was bigger than Ariel, we got along. It was an enduring, not an endearing relationship at best. However, after about two months with Penny and Ariel, Jim decided to move again.

This time he took a room in the home on Pearl Street where he still is the gardener. I couldn't believe I was going back in the old neighborhood, to the tall, narrow brick house, where three other cats were in permanent residence. I was on my best behavior as I was gradually introduced to Isaac Guardian, Jacob Picasso, and Rachael Louise.

Isaac is the senior house cat and he puts on the most superior airs. At ten years of age, he spends most of his time in his own little world. Jacob is mellower. He is a marmalade-colored cat and much leaner than me. He and I became friends after a while and now we take evening walks in the courtyard garden. This year, he is the historian and recording secretary.

And then there is Rachael Louise. Oh, my, what a bossy female she is. Street smart, for sure. She is the only one of us four cats to have claws, and she likes to show them off and give us lessons in how to keep them sharp and use them. Mostly, the grande dame spends her days dozing in a most comfortable armchair in Beth's studio upstairs.

Jim is very good to me. Every morning when the nearby church bell rings six times, he wakes up and says to me.

"Hey, Big Boy, it's time to get up and come out with me while I water the garden." Then he serves me breakfast. He combs me and gives me my morning bath, which oddly enough, I enjoy.

Since we moved back to Pearl Street, we feel very much at home. I inhale fresh air and soak up the sun while I watch Jim take care of the garden. I spy on all kinds of birds while I hide in the ivy-walled courtyard. I flip my tail at squirrels and they flip their tails back. Recently, two new catnip plants have appeared in the garden. What could make me happier than to be curled up beside a small mound of fresh soil next to mint-smelling catnip plants? Who could have put them there?

Yes, you guessed right. My own Jim, the gardener. The courtyard is now so beautiful; thousands of visitors walk through it every year. Beth sits out in the garden and chats with the visitors.

"The garden is lovelier every year. You're lucky to still have Jim, the gardener," many people tell her.

If I'm outside, people point at me and comment, "Look at the size of that big marmalade cat!"

"That's Bubba," Beth says. She always smiles at me and tells people I used to live next door. I purr with happiness when she says, "Hey, Big Boy. We're glad to have you back in the old neighborhood!"

****

A POST SCRIPT FROM JACOB

Sometimes Beth talks about her late husband, Henry, and how he cultivated her interest in cats. It's been a long time since Abner, Jerusha, Blackcat and Queenie went up to the Great Cat in the Sky. Monique still lives in the house with Betty, who continues to help Beth keep the house sparkling. Isaac, Rachael Louise, Bubba, and yours truly, are getting old, fat and lazy. We also doze a lot. Still, we are feeling quite well. Beth has our nine portraits displayed in different rooms throughout the house.

But recently, we were worried, lonely and sad because Beth was in hospital for ten weeks. The house was empty without her, and we missed her more than you can ever imagine. She sent us messages to say friends brought her gifts of toy cats, and she received numerous get-well cards with funny cat poems. Most of all, she sent us messages to tell us that we continue to bring joy to her, and fun into the tall, narrow brick house.

Yours truly,

Jacob Picasso, historian and recording secretary.

March 2008

P. P. S. Sadly, on March 6, 2008, our dear Beth closed her eyes and peacefully went to her eternal reward. J.P.

****

DID YOU KNOW...

According to the Humane Society of the United States: There are between 4,000 and 6,000 animal shelters in the United States. Six to eight million cats and dogs enter shelters each year. Three to four million cats and dogs are euthanized in shelters each year. Three to four million cats and dogs are adopted from shelters each year. Between 600,000 and 750,000 are reclaimed by owners from shelters each year (30% of dogs and 2.5% of cats). A fertile cat can produce three litters in one year. The average number of kittens in a feline litter is four to six.

The purchase of this book will help give a homeless cat a last chance to find a good home.

ABOUT THE AUTHOR

Elizabeth Squire married Henry Deichman in 1963. Besides acquiring each other, they found an old brick house with lots of windows that needed care. They took in Abner O'Grady and Jerusha Killarney because they also needed to be cared for in a good home. Thus began a lifelong love of home and cats.

Elizabeth lived in the tall, narrow brick house for over forty years. She was a retired occupational therapist who designed creative and therapeutic activities for residents living in nursing homes and the elderly living at home. She was deeply concerned about animal welfare, particularly that of cats without homes.

Her late husband, Henry, was a social worker who worked with troubled adolescents in the Buffalo Public Schools.

Born: January 14, 1928. **Died** March 6, 2008.

ABOUT THE EDITOR

Veronica Breen Hogle was born in Waterford, Ireland. She writes true stories about growing up in small towns and villages in Ireland in the 1940s through '60s. Her stories are published in newspapers, magazines and books in Ireland, Canada and the USA.

She has won awards for:
"Christmas In The Village Of The Monks, Of All the Men I've Ever Loved, Pvt. Patrick Walshe's Frayed Old Letter, and Take Me Home to Moscow."

****

Printed in the United States
108952LV00003B/241-243/P